BRAVE
LIKE MOM

BY MONICA ACKER
ILLUSTRATED BY PARAN KIM

beaming books
MINNEAPOLIS

My mom is strong.

She lifts me up with rocket-booster arms
so I can soar through the sky.

She opens the applesauce jar without making a funny face.

She cradles my sister and me and tells us she's sick.
Sicker than bubblegum medicine can fix.

She tries different treatments now, hoping one
day they will make her feel better.

My mom is strong.

My mom is brave.

She saves me from the spiders that sneaky creep into my room.

She eats the mysterious, bumpy veggies from the fresh air market.

She smiles through the needles,
no lollipop required.

She sleeps alone in a hospital bed
after our footsteps fade away.

My mom is brave.

My mom is fierce.

She wrestles with a largemouth bass
that wriggles on the hook.

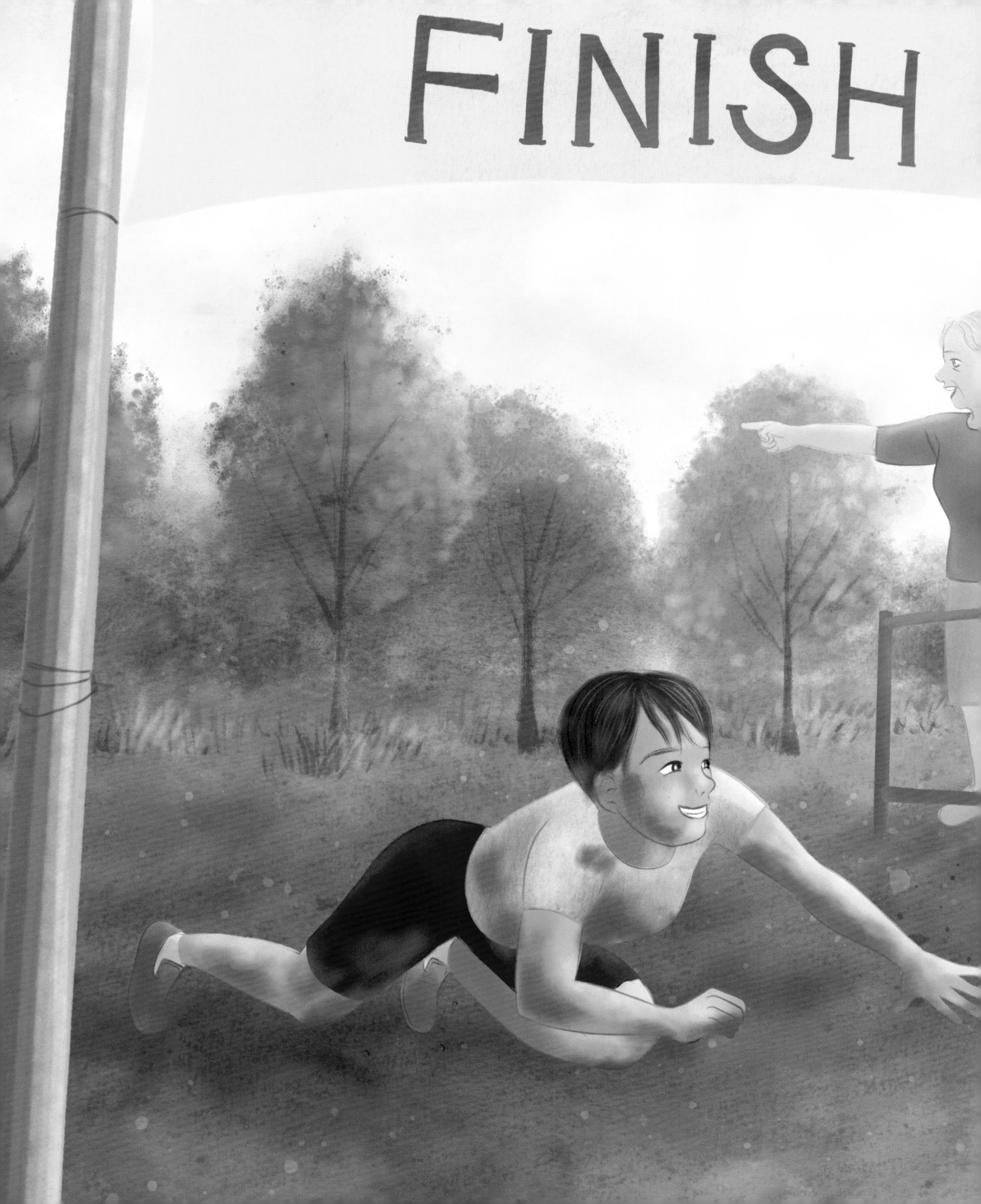
FINISH

She powers through mud puddles
to slide across the finish line.

She fights with every breath she takes
draped in her superhero cape.

She battles fatigue, aches, and pains before
her feet hit the floor each day.

My mom is fierce.

I want to be strong,

to be brave,

to be fierce . . .

like Mom.

But sometimes I'm scared.
Sometimes I cry.

Mom wraps me in a warm hug and tells me being strong doesn't mean you can't cry. Every tear makes the sadness a little lighter.

And being brave doesn't mean you're never scared. Being brave means doing something even when you are scared.

She says we are all fierce warriors pushing through the hard times in hopes of the good stuff to come.

My mom whispers, "You are the strongest, bravest, fiercest kid I know."

I am strong.

I climb rock walls and swing from monkey bars.

I lift my little sister to reach her toothbrush
so Mom can rest a little longer.

I am brave.

I eat the mysterious, mushy meals from friends and neighbors so Mom doesn't have to worry about dinner.

I am fierce.

I am a board game warrior and tic-tac-toe champ.

I battle the bedtime shadows on my own
hoping Mom's kisses will arrive with the sun.

My mom is strong. My mom is brave. My mom is fierce.

And so am I.

AUTHOR'S NOTE

While *Brave Like Mom* is a work of fiction, the real-life, fierce, cancer-fighting mom whose spirit is captured on these pages is my sister-in-law, Nicole. She lit up a room with her smile, her laughter spread like sunshine, she often answered texts with a simple 💪, and she fought for every moment she spent with her girls, defying expectations before succumbing to the disease in January 2020. My sister-in-law was strong and brave and fierce, as are so many families with a loved one battling a life-threatening disease. I wrote this story for Nicole and share it with the hope that everyone who reads this book will be as inspired by her strength and love as all of us who were blessed to know her.

MONICA ACKER is a writer, educator, and mom of three. She holds a BA in Creative Arts and an MAT in Childhood Education. Monica loves to join all of the things: writing groups, book clubs, mom groups, and even Girl Scouts! From 2018 to 2020, Monica watched the strongest person she knows battle cancer and leave a legacy of strength to her two nieces. They are the inspiration for this story.

PARAN KIM grew up in Seoul, South Korea, but moved to Tokyo when she was twenty to study fine art. However, she realized her true passion lay in making picture books, and she became a full-time illustrator. Paran now lives in Dresden, Germany, with her husband.

TO MY STRONG, BRAVE, FIERCE NIECES, ETTA AND NINA —MA

TO THE MEMORY OF MY GRANDMOTHER, WAJU LEE,
WHO TAUGHT ME TO BE BRAVE —PK

27 26 25 24 23 22   1 2 3 4 5 6 7 8

Hardcover ISBN: 978-1-5064-8320-7

Ebook ISBN: 978-1-5064-8321-4

Library of Congress Cataloging-in-Publication Data

Names: Acker, Monica, author. | Kim, Paran, illustrator.
Title: Brave like mom / by Monica Acker ; illustrated by Paran Kim.
Description: Minneapolis : Beaming Books, 2022. | Audience: Ages 5-8. |
Summary: When a young girl's fish-wrestling, spider-wrangling mom
 becomes an illness-fighting mom, they explore together what it means to
 be strong, brave, and fierce.
Identifiers: LCCN 2021057888 (print) | LCCN 2021057889 (ebook) | ISBN
 9781506483207 (hardcover) | ISBN 9781506483214 (ebook)
Subjects: CYAC: Mothers and daughters–Fiction. | Sick–Fiction. | LCGFT:
Picture books.
Classification: LCC PZ7.1.A2234 Br 2022 (print) | LCC PZ7.1.A2234 (ebook)
| DDC [E]–dc23
LC record available at https://lccn.loc.gov/2021057888
LC ebook record available at https://lccn.loc.gov/2021057889

VN0004589; 9781506483207; SEPT2022

Beaming Books
PO Box 1209
Minneapolis, MN 55440-1209
Beamingbooks.com